MW00873105

RIGBY
MAKES A DIFFERENCE

Ruth Zimmerman
Illustrated by Amy Pittman

Make a difference

Ruth Zimmerman

2019

Copyright © 2019 Ruth Zimmerman.

All rights reserved. No part of this book may be used or reproduced by any means,
graphic, electronic, or mechanical, including photocopying, recording, taping or by any
information storage retrieval system without the written permission of the author
except in the case of brief quotations embodied in critical articles and reviews.

Interior Art Credit: Amy Pittman

WestBow Press books may be ordered through booksellers or by contacting:

WestBow Press
A Division of Thomas Nelson & Zondervan
1663 Liberty Drive
Bloomington, IN 47403
www.westbowpress.com
1 (866) 928-1240

Because of the dynamic nature of the Internet, any web addresses or links contained
in this book may have changed since publication and may no longer be valid. The views
expressed in this work are solely those of the author and do not necessarily reflect the
views of the publisher, and the publisher hereby disclaims any responsibility for them.

This is a work of fiction. All of the characters, names, incidents, organizations, and dialogue
in this novel are either the products of the author's imagination or are used fictitiously.

Any people depicted in stock imagery provided by Getty Images are models,
and such images are being used for illustrative purposes only.
Certain stock imagery © Getty Images.

ISBN: 978-1-9736-6748-3 (sc)
ISBN: 978-1-9736-6749-0 (e)

Library of Congress Control Number: 2019908721

Print information available on the last page.

WestBow Press rev. date: 7/11/2019

WESTBOW
PRESS®
A DIVISION OF THOMAS NELSON
& ZONDERVAN

To Will, Drew, Jon, Mary and Sarah – My treasures!
Make a difference! ☺

And to sweet, little Naomi...
You didn't have long, but you *did* make a difference!

Special thanks to my sweet Darling and my children! You've worked so hard throughout the years to create a place for families to make sweet memories together. You've made such a difference in my life and in the lives of countless others!

To Amy, my dear niece, who enthusiastically agreed to take this journey with me. Thank you from the bottom of my heart!

Rigby let out a big contented sigh as he breathed in the warm September air! "Oh man! I just love the fall! How could life possibly be any better than this?"

It was indeed a picture-perfect day at Hickory Creek Farm! The sun blanketed the fields with warmth, and the meadowlarks darted happily amidst the tall grassy meadows. Mr. Z had just finished milking Honey, the brown Jersey cow, and had turned her back out of the barn to munch contentedly on hay.

The Farmer carried the foaming milk bucket into the house where his wife greeted him with a warm smile.

"Looks like Honey did well today! Almost three gallons of milk there! I'll get it put away." Reaching out for the bucket, she began pouring the warm, white liquid into big glass jars before placing them carefully into the refrigerator.

Mr. Z quietly remarked, "I can't believe summer's almost gone already! It'll soon be pumpkin pickin' time! I saw several orange ones in the field this afternoon."

"Lands sakes! How can it be? Seems like we just planted them yesterday!" exclaimed his wife.

The Farmer nodded his head. "Yesterday? More like three months ago! Would you like to stroll out to the pumpkin patch with me? I thought you might like to pick out a few for the front porch."

"I'd like that!" his wife replied. Hand in hand, they headed out the front door, making their way around the tall, concrete silo beside the barn before coming to the four-acre pumpkin patch just beyond.

Rigby, a little mini pumpkin about the size of a man's palm, lay snuggled amidst the giant green leaves and vines that twisted around and around. He spied the middle-aged couple as they headed his direction and overheard them discussing which pumpkins might look just right for the fall display that would soon grace their front porch.

"Oh, pick me! Pick me!" thought Rigby. Why, he would love to decorate the porch of the two-story white farmhouse with the green shutters. Everyone who came to the farm would see him there and marvel at how beautiful he was! Surely, there could be nothing that would make him happier!

Although he could barely contain his excitement at the thought, the little mini pumpkin patiently waited. The farmer's wife pointed to a nice big, round pumpkin just two rows from Rigby and remarked, "Why there's a beautiful one! And the one right next to it would be perfect beside it!" Mr. Z took a pair of clippers from the pocket of his jeans and stooped down to cut the stems of the chosen ones. He stood and gently placed the smaller of the two in his wife's arms. He then bent down once more to pick up the second one. Together they headed back to the house with their treasures.

Rigby sighed, "Maybe next time!"

A whole week went by and Rigby patiently lay in his soft bed of vines in the pumpkin patch. The pumpkins were ripening nicely, with fewer and fewer green ones and more and more orange ones as time passed.

He began to hear excited voices. The Martin family from the next farm over had just arrived. Mr. and Mrs. Martin, along with their three young children, began making their way down the first row of pumpkins.

He heard Mr. Martin tell his children, "Look them all over very carefully! Decide which pumpkin you like the very best and then we'll pick it."

Eight-year-old Mary Martin immediately spied a medium sized Cinderella pumpkin at the edge of the patch and bent down next to it. She excitedly motioned for her dad to come help her clip the stem.

Rigby watched as twelve-year-old Drew Martin headed for the really big pumpkins planted at the far end of the patch. He quickly eyed a big orange one with wrinkles and claimed it as his own.

Four-year-old Will Martin walked hand in hand with his mom. As they made their way up and down the rows, she would suggest first one then another to her son. He shook his head again and again. "Nope! That's not it! It's got to be perfect!"

Suddenly, Will broke free from his mom and squealed with delight as he headed toward a beautiful Cannonball pumpkin. As the name implies, it was about the size of a cannonball, perfectly round with a nice dark stem.

Mrs. Martin gazed at the orange ball, remarking to her young son what a great choice he'd made. "It's just the right size for you to carry all by yourself!"

Rigby watched as the Martins loaded their treasures into their blue mini-van. They enthusiastically discussed what type of face they planned to carve into their pumpkins. And then they were gone, leaving a trail of dust behind them as they disappeared down the drive.

Rigby tried to be brave. "They did pick some nice pumpkins. Maybe next time it'll be my turn."

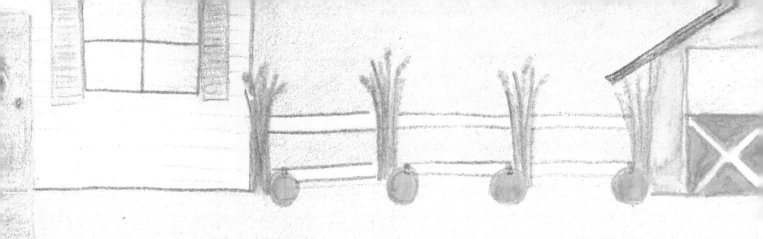

The last Saturday of September was an extra special one at Hickory Creek Farm! It was opening day! Promptly at 1:00 p.m., Mr. Z swung open the green metal gate, welcoming customers to his farm.

Throughout the afternoon, Rigby watched in amazement as lots and lots of families strolled through the pumpkin patch in search of their perfect pumpkin.

HICKORY CREEK FARM

Rigby held his breath as a little girl with long yellow curls stooped down to smile at him. "I like this one, Mommy! He's so cute!"

The little girl's mother kindly agreed with her daughter and then remarked, "It is awfully cute, Sarah, but it's really too small for carving. Why don't you see if you can find a bigger one?"

A big tear dropped down Rigby's cheek as he watched the little girl move on down the path. Would no one *ever* pick him?

Monday dawned sunshiny and bright. "What a perfect day!" Rigby beamed. "Surely today will be *my* day!" He spied a big yellow school bus pulling into the parking lot beside the driveway. One by one, he watched as twenty kindergarteners from the nearby town filed down the steps. "Wow!" thought Rigby. "I've never seen so many kids all at once!"

The children disappeared into the giant eighty-year-old barn that stood majestically beside the pumpkin patch. Mrs. Z welcomed them heartily. She carefully described to them how pumpkins grow from a seed to a grown-up pumpkin.

The children could hardly contain their
excitement as they exited the barn. First, they
stood together at Honey's pen. Mrs. Z pointed to
her old jersey cow, explaining to the class, "That's
where your milk comes from."

She then led them to attached pens, introducing the boys and girls to
her goats, Salt and Pepper. The children giggled as the goats ran up the
ramp and peered at them from atop their house.

In the next pen, Buster the sheep gazed at them from under the shady pecan tree while trying to stay cool. The sun was just a bit too warm for his liking.

Then came Whinny the miniature horse and Eyore the mini donkey. The kids laughed when Eyore brayed for them, "Awww! Eeeee Awwwww!"

Mrs. Z continued along the row of enclosures, explaining where we get eggs from as they stood in front of the chicken pen. The children loved watching the ducks swim in the little pond on the other side of the fence. And then came the baby pigs. Tic, Tac, and Toe napped contentedly in the shade while the children gazed at them through the fence.

Rigby's heart skipped a beat when he heard Mrs. Z instruct the children that it was time for them to pick their very own mini pumpkin to take home. "Look all the way down the row before you decide which one's the very best! Then pick one!"

Rigby's heart was pounding as he watched the children venture up and down the row in which he was planted. One by one each kindergartener made his selection, tearing it from the vine and squealing with delight as he headed back to his teacher.

And then they were gone! Poor Rigby cried with great disappointment. No one had picked him!

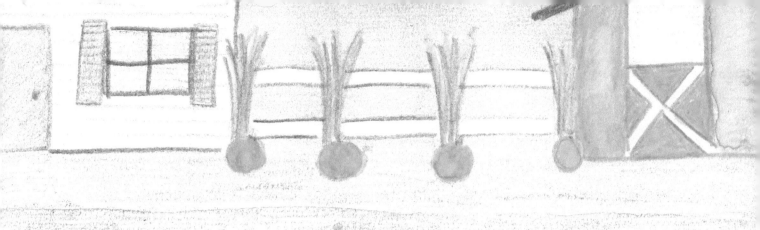

Day after day went by as October slipped away. Families came and went. Each time a yellow school bus pulled into the parking lot, Rigby's hopes grew, only to be dashed again as he'd watch it drive away.

Then the day came when Mr. and Mrs. Z stood at the front gate after hanging up the big "CLOSED" sign.

"Oh no! The pumpkin patch is closed! And nobody picked me!" cried little Rigby! He had wanted so much to bring happiness to someone! He wanted to be special! That night was indeed a gloomy one for the mini pumpkin. He had never been so dejected in all his short life!

November 1st dawned a bit cloudy, perfect for little Rigby's cloudy mood! He was surprised to see the farmer and his wife heading out to the pumpkin patch. Mr. Z carried a faded bushel basket under one arm. He instructed his wife, "Get a nice assortment. You point to the ones you want, and I'll pick them for you."

Mrs. Z began strolling down the row of mini pumpkins. One by one she pointed. Her husband would then stoop down and pick, placing the chosen little pumpkins into his basket. Rigby's eyes grew wide as the farmer's wife pointed right at him. "Now there's a nice one. I'm glad he's still here!"

Mr. Z bent down, clipping Rigby's green stem. The farmer gently placed him in the basket. The little pumpkin's heart was pounding! "I wonder where they're taking me! I thought pumpkin season was over!"

The farmer and his wife filled the basket to the top before carefully placing it into the bed of their old red pickup. "Here we go!" remarked Mr. Z as he put the key into the ignition.

The old truck headed out to Highway 47, then on to the little town just ten miles away. Rigby nervously waited as the truck pulled up in front of a long, flat building. Mr. Z turned off the engine then carefully picked up the basket and headed through the big front doors.

That night at dinner, Rigby found himself in the middle of a dining room table. He was tucked cozily beside some of his friends in a cute little basket. He watched as a gray-haired man pushed his walker toward the table. He looked troubled, a vacant stare in his gray eyes. The old man awkwardly slumped into the chair and lowered his head, waiting for his dinner to arrive.

Rigby's heart went out to the old man, longing to make his day better. He could think of nothing that would be better than to make this poor man smile.

"Here's your dinner, Jon! Enjoy!" instructed a lady wearing a powder blue uniform. She placed a tray in front of the old man and turned to serve someone at the next table.

Suddenly, the man reached for his napkin. He spied the wicker basket of mini pumpkins in the center of his table with Rigby right on the top. The man's mind wondered back to his farm. He had grown up there and then raised his family there. He had picked many pumpkins in the garden beside his shuttered farm house. He smiled dreamily as he remembered.

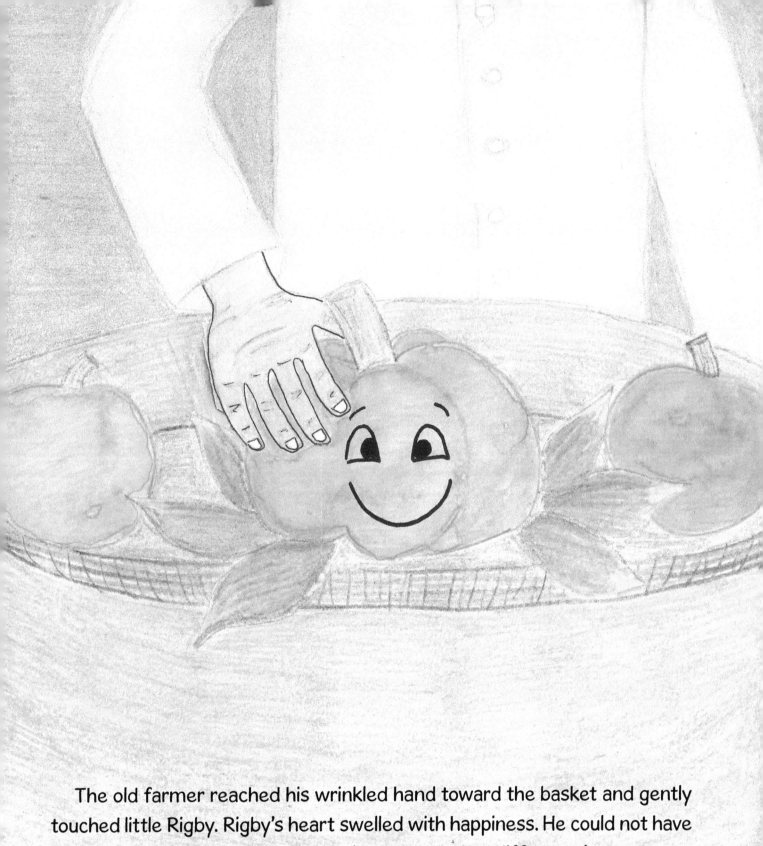

The old farmer reached his wrinkled hand toward the basket and gently touched little Rigby. Rigby's heart swelled with happiness. He could not have chosen a better place to have gone! He had made a difference!

Think About It!

1. What color is a pumpkin before it turns orange?
2. What kind of pumpkin did Will pick?
3. What were the Martin children going to do with their pumpkins?
4. What did Eyore the mini donkey say?
5. What made Rigby really happy?
6. How can *you* make a difference in someone's life today?

CPSIA information can be obtained
at www.ICGtesting.com
Printed in the USA
BVHW020535180719
553735BV00002B/5/P

9 781973 667483